My Shoes Got the Blues

Brian Davis 79 pgs.

Illustrations by Ron Wheeler

McRuffy Press 2003

To my wife and children.
You never cease to inspire me.

My Shoes Got the Blues

Published by McRuffy Press
PO Box 212
Raymore, Missouri 64083

Story by Brian Davis
Illustrations by Ron Wheeler
Cover design and illustrations by Ron Wheeler

ISBN 1-59269-057-2

www.McRuffy.com

Contents

Chapter 1

The Trouble Begins

"Buster! Buster!" called Matthew. "Where is that dog?" Then, Matthew noticed the pile of dirt by the fence. "Buster!" Matthew yelled louder as he ran toward the dirt.

Just as he reached the fence, Buster poked his head out of a hole. The pup had dug a tunnel under the wooden fence. A big yellow onion was in Buster's mouth.

"Oh no! Mr. Johnson's vegetable garden!" said Matthew in horror.

Matthew thought of the few times his soccer

ball had sailed over the fence. The ball once landed three feet from the garden. Mr. Johnson refused to give the ball back to him. He said Matthew's father would have to ask for it back.

No one in the neighborhood talked to Mr. Johnson. He was always angry with someone or something. Matthew's neighbor was at least seventy years old. His thin gray hair and dark crinkled face didn't hide his age.

"This is not good...not good at all," sighed Matthew. "Mr. Johnson will probably call the dog pound when he sees this."

Matthew thought for moment. Buster dropped the onion and licked his hand.

"Onion breath!" Matthew winced.

He walked to the garden shed at the back of their yard. Inside he found what he was looking for. Matthew used a shovel to fill in the dirt. Buster tried to help by digging it out again.

"No!" commanded Matthew. He grabbed the dog's collar and tied him to the leash. "You're in enough trouble as it is." Buster whimpered and sat down.

Next, Matthew set a ladder up to the fence. He grabbed the onion and stepped on the ladder. Crack! The top six inches of the fence board broke. Matthew's heart sank.

"I'll fix it later,' he mumbled.

Finally, he reached the top of the fence. Matthew tossed the onion and jumped. Rip! His pants pocket caught on the splintered fence. The pocket flapped in the breeze.

"Great! Just great!" Matthew said angrily.

He looked around the yard. No one was watching. Matthew spotted the place where Buster had launched his attack. Two rows of the garden looked terrible. Several plants lay scattered around. Matthew quickly "replanted" the vegetables. The garden just didn't look the same. Some of the tomato plants had already started to wilt. A green pepper was knocked off the stem. All Matthew could do was brush over the puppy prints.

Just then, the sound of an electric garage door opener startled Matthew.

"Mr. Johnson!" thought Matthew in horror.

He looked toward the gate. It was locked. Matthew noticed the apple tree at the back corner of the lot. A limb hung over another neighbor's fence.

Matthew climbed the tree and edged himself out on the limb. Crack! The limb broke and Matthew tumbled to the ground. Matthew was in the next yard laying face down.

"Grrr!"

The sound had woken the sleeping bulldog. The dog stepped from its doghouse on the opposite side of the yard. Matthew sprang to his feet and ran for the gate.

Too late! The dog beat him to the gate and stood there. The dog bared his teeth and snarled. Matthew quickly looked around for anything to fight off the dog.

He grabbed a bucket and tossed it at the dog. That's when it happened. The bucket landed a foot from the dog on the concrete sidewalk.

The lid popped off and bright blue paint

spilled out. The bright blue bulldog ran for his house. Matthew ran for the gate, stepping in the paint. Bright blue tennis shoe prints marked Matthew's race to the street.

Matthew was completely out of breath when he reached his own yard. That's when Matthew remembered the ladder. He grabbed it and raced for the garden shed. He was carefully placing the ladder back on a rack his father had made.

Chapter 2

More Trouble

"My garden!" Mr. Johnson yelled from the other side of the fence.

Matthew jumped and fell off balance still holding the ladder. The other end of the ladder spun. Crack! "Ohhhh!" The end of the ladder poked through the window of the garden shed.

Matthew heard Mr. Johnson tromp back into his house. All of the sudden, Matthew remembered the broken board on the fence. He ran to the place he had climbed over. He looked for the broken piece. It was nowhere around. Matthew realized it must have fallen on Mr. Johnson's side of the fence.

Matthew jumped up and down trying to see over the fence. He didn't want to use the ladder again. Matthew ran and got a metal garbage can to stand on. He carefully climbed on the can. The broken piece of board was laying right on the dirt Buster had dug.

Just then the metal lid of the garbage can bent. Matthew sank into a bag of garbage.

"Yuck!" cried Matthew as garbage oozed over his Double Pump Slammers. "My good shoes!"

The can tipped over and Matthew stumbled out. He tried to put the lid back on the can. The lid was bent at an angle in the center.

"I'll fix it later," thought Matthew.

Matthew knew he couldn't climb over the fence to get the broken piece. He went back to the garden shed and got the shovel. Matthew began digging under the fence. He wanted to hurry so Mr. Johnson wouldn't catch him.

The shovel struck a rock. It firmly wedged between the rock and fence. Matthew forced the handle of the shovel down. Crack! The handle snapped off of the metal blade.

"Oh no!" sighed Matthew.

The blade was still stuck. Matthew walked over to Buster. He unsnapped the leash and led the dog to the fence.

"Dig, Buster!"

Buster joyfully uncovered the hole he had created earlier. Matthew reached under the fence and found the broken board. He then quickly filled in the hole using his hands.

"Now how can I fix the fence?" Matthew asked Buster. The pup just panted happily. "You're not much help," said Matthew. "I need

some glue...hmm."

Matthew walked back to the garden shed. He found a bottle of wood glue on the shelf. The glue had dried around the cap. Matthew could not get it open. He grabbed a pair of pliers and sat down in the doorway.

He was able to twist the whole spout off. Matthew poured the glue on the freshly broken edge of the board. He set the glue bottle down. Matthew walked back toward the fence. Buster walked to the garden shed and sniffed the glue.

The pup put one paw up to the bottle and it tipped. Glue flowed over the floor and onto the door. Buster thought the bottle would make a great chew toy. He carried it away with glue dripping everywhere.

Matthew was busy back at the fence. He

carefully placed the broken piece of wood back onto the fence. Matthew backed up a few feet. He squinted his eyes. Matthew tilted his head.

"No one will ever notice," Matthew said to himself as he admired his handiwork.

Matthew decided it was time for a snack. He went into the house. He poured a large glass of lemonade. After drinking it, he went to his room and read a comic book.

A squirrel running along the wooden fence was in for a surprise. The furry little animal jumped right onto the freshly repaired board. A piece toppled into the yard. The surprised squirrel also toppled into the yard.

"A visitor!" Buster seemed to think as he began to chase the squirrel.

The squirrel ran to the garden shed for cover. Buster was sure the squirrel wanted to play tag. He followed the squirrel. Buster barked happily as the squirrel scrambled from wall to wall.

The squirrel scrambled up the walls. It hopped onto shelves. Cans of nails, bolts, and nuts spilled everywhere. Paint cans toppled and tools fell to the floor. Buster was having a great time.

Back on the fence, a tired bird found a nice place to rest. The little sparrow had no idea that the white stuff at its feet was glue. It just stood on the fence and chirped happily. The bird sang its lovely song. It watched the squirrel jump from the broken window of the tool shed.

Buster's newfound friend was gone. He was sad for a couple of minutes. Then, he realized the squirrel had knocked over a lot of new toys for him to play with. Buster sank his teeth into a wooden handle of a hammer and dragged it outside.

Chapter 3

Animal Control

The happy pup found a good place to bury the hammer. Buster had to dig a hole under the fence first. Right next to the onions in Mr. Johnson's garden seemed like the perfect place to hide his prize. Now he had to find places for the rest of the tools.

"There's an animal control truck in Mr. Johnson's driveway!" Rachel yelled to her mom.

Matthew had been reading for about thirty minutes. He jumped off his bed. He ran into the hallway.

"Oh no! Buster!" he yelled.

His mother stepped out of the family room. "Matthew, Mr. Johnson doesn't have any reason to do anything to Buster."

She looked at Matthew. "...or does he?"

"How would I know?" asked Matthew. Matthew glanced out the window into the backyard. Buster was asleep under the tree.

"I guess he doesn't."

But then Matthew noticed something else. Mr. Johnson and two other men were doing something by the fence. Matthew stared and turned pale.

His mother looked out the window. "What are they doing?"

"I'll find out!" said Rachel as she ran out the door.

Her mom didn't wait for her. She followed Rachel out into the yard. Matthew felt sick. He felt dizzy. He felt like he wished this day had never happened. Matthew followed his mother and sister outside.

"Mom, a sparrow is stuck to our fence," said Rachel.

"What?" Mrs. Day looked at Mr. Johnson. "How did this happen?"

"It looks like glue," snarled Mr. Johnson.

"Somebody glued a sparrow to the fence? Mr. Johnson, I find that hard to believe!"

"Tell it to the sparrow," answered Mr. Johnson.

"Hey, what's going on?" It was Matthew's dad. He had just gotten home from work.

"Mr. Johnson glued a sparrow to the fence!" said Rachel.

"I did not," denied Mr. Johnson. "If I had to blame anyone, I'd blame that pup over there."

Everyone turned and looked at Buster. He had the empty glue bottle in his mouth. He was waiting for someone to take it and play catch. Leaves and sticks were stuck in dried glue all over his fur.

"Buster, you're a mess," Matthew's father shook his head. "I know this dog can't climb fences. I think he had help."

He looked right at Matthew. The animal control workers almost had the sparrow free. A voice came over their radio. One of the workers put it up to his mouth and answered the call.

"A bright, blue, bulldog?"

"Yeah, we're pretty close to there, I think." He put the radio down to his chest. "Hey Bob, how far are we from 1094 Oak Street?"

Before the other worker could answer, Mr. Johnson spoke up. "1094 Oak Street, that's right in back of my yard!"

The sparrow fluttered free. Mr. Johnson and the two men walked to the back of the yard. They peeked over the fence. Looking back at them was a bulldog that had been painted blue.

"Hey, how did this limb get broken?" asked Mr. Johnson looking at the apple tree.

"My garden shed!" yelled Mr. Day. He saw the broken window, the scattered tools, and the mess of nuts and bolts. It looked like a tornado had struck.

"This definitely looks like gang activity." One of the animal control workers said. "I can call the police on my radio."

"Police!" yelled Matthew. "No don't!"

His parents looked at him.

"Talk, Matthew," said his father.

Matthew told the whole story. At least he told as much of it as he knew. He wasn't sure how the sparrow ended up on the fence. Gluing the fence was enough for him to be blamed for that.

He even had to add the parts his family hadn't found yet. The bent trash can, the broken shovel, the list just didn't seem to end. When he finished the story everyone was silent.

Finally, Mr. Johnson put his hand to his mouth. At first he just snickered. His face turned red and he laughed, hard and loud.

Nobody had ever seen Mr. Johnson laugh. One by one everyone joined in laughing, except Matthew. It just didn't seem too funny to him.

"Matthew's reign of terror!" laughed one of the animal control officers.

That night Matthew's father made a few phone calls. He called Mr. Johnson. He called

the Anderson's. They were the people who had the blue dog.

Matthew was happy his dad was taking care of everything. At least, Matthew thought his dad was taking care of everything.

"Well Matthew," said his father after talking to everyone on the phone. "You're going to be very busy the next few Saturdays."

Chapter 4

Paying the Price

Matthew's father had worked everything out. Matthew would do a number of jobs to make up for everything.

Several weeks of Matthew's allowance would pay for things. He would buy a window, garbage can, blue paint, and a shovel.

The next Saturday morning would be spent scrubbing the Anderson's sidewalk. Saturday afternoon he would work in Mr. Johnson's garden. The Anderson's agreed to take care of cleaning their dog. They didn't think it would like seeing Matthew again.

His father had a lot of work for him to do in his own yard. Cleaning the garden shed would be his first job. Mr. Day was even making Matthew build a bird feeder. He thought Matthew owed something to the sparrows. Matthew would also have to replace the board in the fence. First he had to find the hammer.

Saturday morning went well. The paint

cleaned up easier than he thought. The Andersons were pleased. It was the afternoon that Matthew wasn't looking forward to.

He was still a little afraid of Mr. Johnson.

After lunch, Matthew was very tense as he rang the doorbell. Mr. Johnson opened the door suddenly. Matthew jumped back. The old man was dressed in garden clothes.

Mr. Johnson looked at his watch, "Right on time. Are you ready to work?"

Mr. Johnson told him to go through the gate. Matthew's first job would be pulling weeds. Matthew walked to the garden. Mr. Johnson had a huge garden. It looked like he had left it all for Matthew to weed.

"I'll never get all this done!" Matthew said to himself.

Mr. Johnson came out the door. He carried a water jug and two cups.

"We'll work up a thirst today! You start in the tomatoes. I'll start with the potatoes. We'll meet at the onions." He laughed.

Matthew smiled a little. Mr. Johnson didn't seem nearly as mean as Matthew had thought.

Matthew weeded the tomatoes. Then he began to help Mr. Johnson with the onions.

"What's this?" said Mr. Johnson as he dug around an onion. He tugged on a piece of wood.

"Our hammer!" said Matthew. "Buster must have buried it."

Mr. Johnson pulled it out of the dirt. The onion came out with it. He handed the hammer to Matthew and held the onion in his hands.

"Let's take a break."

Mr. Johnson set up a couple of lawn chairs. They sat under a shade tree. Mr. Johnson poured a glass of water for Matthew. He then poured one for himself. He took a drink.

"Ahh...nothing like a cool drink on a hot afternoon."

Matthew looked over the garden. "Isn't this an awfully large garden for one person? You must really like vegetables."

Mr. Johnson laughed as he juggled the onion in his hands. "I give most of it away to the food pantry." Matthew never thought of Mr. Johnson doing anything nice. "I just enjoy watching things grow. I don't mind helping other people out, too."

They were both quiet for awhile. Finally, Mr. Johnson asked, "Why did you do it?"

"Do what?" asked Matthew.

"Terrorize the neighborhood instead of telling the truth."

"I was afraid, I guess," answered Matthew.

"Afraid of the truth," said Mr. Johnson. "My, my...Matthew, lying is like an onion."

"An onion?"

Mr. Johnson picked off the top layer of the onion. "If you tell one lie, you have to tell another."

"Oh," said Matthew. "If you peel off one layer of onion, there's another underneath."

"Right," said Mr. Johnson, "and another, and another. If you smell an onion, your eyes get blurry. Just like a lie keeps you from seeing clearly."

"It sure is a lot easier to tell the truth. Even though it seems hard at the time. I guess that's why the Bible tells us to be truthful," said Matthew.

"I don't know about the Bible," said Mr. Johnson. "But it sure would be easier on the animals around here."

Up in the tree, a sparrow whistled an "amen".

Chapter 5

Double Pump Slammers

"This is Radio KRUF. We're waiting for the right answer to today's question. What kind of shoes does the superstar basketball player, Sky Bordon, wear?"

Matthew couldn't believe it. His fingers stumbled over each other as he called the number. The line was ringing,

"You're on Radio KRUF and it's your turn to answer."

"Uh..," Matthew almost forgot the answer. "Double Sump Plammers...I mean Double Pump Slammers."

"You're exactly right! What is the name of our big winner?" asked the announcer.

"My name is Matthew Day."

"You sound kind of young Matt. Let me guess your age. I'd say you're about eight."

"I'm nine," corrected Matthew.

"Well, you've won a poster of Sky Bordon wearing his Double Pump Slammers. You've also won tickets to a Stingray's basketball game. Don't forget, you'll be entered into our grand prize contest. Well, we have to go to a commercial. Matthew, stay on the line. We need to get your name and address."

Matthew gave the radio station all the facts they needed. He then ran up the stairs to his parent's room.

"Dad! Dad! I won!"

His father had just finished shaving. "Won what?"

"I answered the KRUF question of the day. I won two tickets to a Stingray's game. I also won a Sky Bordon poster."

"That's great Matthew," smiled his dad as he patted him on the back. "Hey, who are you taking to the game?" Mr. Day hinted.

Matthew smiled, "I haven't decided...Mom or Rachel."

"Tough decision, Matthew. Kind of like the

decision I have to make. Do I give you an allowance or not?" teased his dad.

"Are you free next Friday night?" asked Matthew.

"I might be going to a basketball game," answered his father.

"I have two tickets," said Matthew.

"Great! Bring your allowance. You can buy the hot dogs!" said his father.

"Don't push it Dad," laughed Matthew as he left the room.

Matthew was excited as he got on the bus.

"Hi Rail!" he called to his friend.

"I heard!" said Rail.

"How?" asked Matthew.

"I heard you on the radio. You're famous," said Rail.

"Hey, Day, are you wearing your Double Sump Plammers?" One of the older boys teased Matthew.

"They're just jealous," said Rail. Matthew

sank down in his seat.

His friends at school were excited. They asked him if he got nervous talking on the radio.

"Not at all!" he said. "I was just making a joke with the Double Sump Plammers."

Matthew then remembered he should never lie.

"Okay, I was very nervous." Matthew promised to bring his poster of Sky Bordon to school.

He couldn't wait until Friday. It seemed like his father couldn't wait either.

A car horn honked. "Hey Matthew!"

Matthew had just started walking toward the bus after school. His father was sitting in the car. Matthew grabbed the strap on his backpack. He jogged to the car.

"Hi Dad! Why are you here?"

Honk!

"Hey, Rachel!" Rachel also ran to the car.

Their father explained, "I thought we'd go by the radio station. I don't want to take any chances with those tickets. They could get lost in the mail. I called them this morning. I said we would be by to pick them up."

"Alright, I'll get my poster today! Sky Bordon, he's the greatest!" said Matthew.

Chapter 6

KRUF-AM

The radio station was located outside the city. They drove for about twenty minutes. The tall broadcast tower rose a few miles ahead.

"Wow, a real radio station!" said Rachel. At the foot of the tower was a small red brick building. Big stainless steel letters, KRUF, marked the building.

"Mr. Day?" asked the secretary.

"How did you know?" asked Mr. Day.

"I talked to you on the phone. We don't get many visitors out here." She looked at Matthew. "You must be the big winner, Matthew, right?"

Rachel was busy looking around the station. It was actually very small. There were three large desks in the lobby. Two were empty.

The secretary was sitting at the third. A door that read "Joy Hansen, Manager" was on the left. Another door led to what looked like a meeting room. There were also a couple of rest rooms and a closet.

A man behind a thick glass window swayed to some music. A light was on next to the words, "On the air". There was a second room with a glass window on the far right. Between the two rooms was another door that read, "Control Room".

"Where's the rest of the radio station?" asked Rachel.

"This is it!" laughed the secretary. Then the telephone rang, "Good afternoon, KRUF-AM. How can I help you?" said the secretary.

"She's not in at the moment. Can I take a message?" She grabbed a pen and paper. The secretary wrote a name and telephone number.

She started writing a message, then stopped.

"He can't do that!" The secretary spoke into the telephone. "Sky promised...he can't...He gave his word."

"She must be talking about Sky Bordon," whispered Matthew to his dad. A nice looking woman in a business suit walked through the doorway.

The secretary waved the woman over to her. The woman picked up the telephone receiver.

"This is Joy Hansen...I see...Please tell Mr. Bordon's agent that he made a promise. He wouldn't want to make his fans think he is a liar. I'll hold..." The woman just shook her head and frowned at the secretary. "I thought he'd see it our way." Joy smiled and hung up the phone.

"Is Sky still going to do the contest?" asked the secretary. "He'd better. We've got an advertisement in the newspaper tomorrow. He gave us his word. We didn't make him do this."

Mrs. Hansen noticed the Day family.

"Sorry about that. We just got a little distracted. I'm Joy Hansen, the station manager. You must be Matthew." She opened a desk drawer and pulled out an envelope. "Here's your tickets."

The secretary went to the closet and pulled out a cardboard tube.

"Here's your poster, Matthew. I hope you enjoy it."

Chapter 7

The Big Game

Matthew was in deep thought on the way home. He was trying to decide the perfect place for the poster.

"I think I'll put it on my door. I can look at it when I go to sleep. He's the greatest!"

His father cleared his throat. "Did I ever tell you about the game I played in? I scored thirty points against East High School."

"Wasn't that the only game you played in Dad?" asked Rachel.

"Yes, but that was a big win for our team," said Mr. Day.

"Mom said it was the only win for your team," said Matthew.

"Well, I got injured after that and missed the last two games of the season. Anyway, I had a mean hook shot. I can show it to you, Matt, if you'd like." Matthew's father offered.

"Okay...sometime," said Matthew. Mr. Day smiled and patted Matthew on the back.

"Have you seen Sky's hook shot? Talk about mean!" said Matthew. Mr. Day gritted his teeth

and stared at the road.

Matthew ran to his room when he got home. He pulled the poster out of the tube. He looked at his door. A white marker board hung on the door. His scripture memory verse was written on the board. *1 John 5:21 Children keep yourselves away from idols.*

"I'll find a place for this somewhere else," he said to himself.

Matthew hung the poster over the scripture verse. He put a plastic basketball hoop above it. Now he could play Sky one-on-one.

Matthew's father knocked on the door, "Wanna shoot some hoops?"

"Uh...not right now," answered Matthew. "I'm a little tired."

His father walked away. Mr. Day could hear the little foam basketball hit the rim.

"He shoots...he scores...Sky Bordon has done it again," yelled Matthew.

"Hooray for Sky," grumbled Mr. Day as he walked to the kitchen.

"Are you O.K.?" Mrs. Day asked Mr. Day.

"I think Matthew is getting too caught up in basketball," he answered.

"Why do you say that?" asked Mrs. Day.

"He only talked about one thing all day, Sky Bordon. He won't even play basketball with me."

"I thought you said he was too caught up in basketball," said Mrs. Day.

"Well, I mean..." began Mr. Day.

"You mean you're jealous of Sky Bordon," said Mrs. Day.

"Wanna shoot a few hoops?" asked Mr. Day.

"Sure," answered Mrs. Day. "Can you teach me to shoot like Sky Bordon?"

"That's it, loser fixes supper!" said Mr. Day.

An hour and a half later, Matthew and Sky had won. It was a double overtime, last second shot, playoff win. The poster on the door made the imaginary game seem real.

"Dinner's ready!" called his mom.

Rachel was setting the table. "Why did Dad cook supper?" she asked.

"My jump shot was working," laughed Mrs. Day. Mr. Day set a pizza on the table. "No one cooks a frozen pizza like you dear," said Mrs. Day.

"Just bless the food and eat," grumbled Mr. Day.

Matthew came into the room. "Frozen pizza? Did Dad cook supper?"

Rachel and Mrs. Day laughed. "Anything wrong with it?" asked Mr. Day.

"No," said Matthew. "Sky Bordon eats this kind of pizza all the time!" Mr. Day suddenly lost his appetite.

On Thursday, Mr. Day bought Matthew a new baseball.

"A baseball, thanks Dad, but it's basketball season," said Matthew.

"We don't have to be like the rest of the world. If we want to play baseball, we can play baseball," explained Mr. Day.

"Sure, Dad," said Matthew. "Are you feeling okay?"

"I feel great," said Mr. Day. "How about a game of catch?"

"Okay," said Matthew.

Matthew went to his room. He tossed the ball on his bed. In the closet, he found his mitt and old baseball. His dad was waiting in the backyard. Mr. Day was tossing sticks for Buster to chase.

Matthew tossed the ball to his dad. "This is your old baseball," said Mr. Day. "Where's the new one?"

He wound his arm back to throw. "I thought I'd save it. Maybe Sky Bordon will autograph it," answered Matthew.

The ball sailed out of Mr. Day's hand. Matthew jumped as high as he could. Crash! The ball broke the new window of the garden shed.

"Wow, I don't think Sky Bordon could have

caught that!" yelled Matthew.

Mr. Day threw down his glove, "Game over."

Matthew's dad marched in the house. Matthew followed. Mr. Day grabbed the newspaper and started to read. Ten seconds later he threw down the paper.

"I guess I'll go out and fix the window."

Matthew picked up the paper. He looked at a full-page ad.

KRUF and Double Pump Slammers presents the Sky's The Limit Stingray Shootout. Tomorrow night. Grand Prize: A day with Sky Bordon!

"Wow," thought Matthew. "A day with Sky Bordon!"

Chapter 8

And The Winner Is...

Finally the big night arrived. Matthew's father was quiet as he parked the car. People were lined up outside the arena.

"Thanks for bringing me," said Matthew.

"What's a dad for?" answered Mr. Day. "Thanks for the ticket."

The crowd was excited. The Stingrays were playing better than they had all year. Sky Bordon led the team to a twenty-five-point lead by halftime. The teams went into the locker rooms. Some cheerleaders from a local high school danced on the floor.

Two men and a woman walked to the center of the court. One of them held a microphone.

"Joy Hansen of KRUF radio will draw the names of our finalist. If your name is called come on down. You could win the Sky's The Limit Stingray Shootout."

"The first name is...Ida Jones. The second name is...Mack Shimlet. The third name is...Matthew Day."

Matthew jumped out of his seat.

"That's me! That's me!" he shouted.

The people around him started applauding.

"Go get'um son," said a lady in front of him.

"Dad, come with me," said Matthew. He tried to catch his breath.

The three contestants lined up on the court. Ida was a short lady in her sixties. Mack was a tough looking man with big muscles. He had a tatoo of a red dragon on his arm. Matthew stood at the end of the line, shaking.

He looked around at all the people. Matthew

could just imagine what it was like to be a pro basketball player. He could just imagine how Sky Bordon felt. It had to feel great to be famous.

All the fans loved him. Of course, Matthew knew that Sky Bordon had to love being a part of the Stingrays. They were the greatest basketball team that Matthew had ever seen. Now it was Matthew's chance to be on the same court where Sky Bordon played.

The rules of the contest were simple. The three would take turns shooting free throws. Each person got three turns. Whoever made the most, won.

Ida went first. She held the ball down by her knees, closed her eyes, and threw. Swish! It was a perfect shot. The crowd cheered. Everyone was surprised, especially Ida.

Mack shot next. He dribbled the ball on the court first. Matthew could feel the floor shake. Mack stared at the basket and threw. The ball fell two feet short.

"Air ball! Air Ball!" shouted the crowd.

Mack grabbed another basketball and threw it at the basket. It hit the front of the rim and bounced back at him. Mack grew angrier. He tossed it once more. The ball flew up into the stands. Mack stomped back to his seat.

Matthew was next. The basket seemed taller down on the court. The hoop seemed a lot smaller. Sweat gathered on his eyebrow. He aimed at the basket.

The ball sailed higher and higher. It hit the rim. The ball spun around and around and fell in.

"Yes!" yelled Matthew. The crowd cheered. Ida patted him on the head.

Ida's second shot slipped from her hands. It never got more than four feet off the ground. The crowd clapped politely. She took a little bow.

Matthew's second shot was better than his first. It swooshed through the basket. If Ida missed her next shot, Matthew would be the winner. Ida walked up to the line. She turned and winked at Matthew.

Her shot flew completely over the backboard.

"The Grand Prize winner is Matthew Day." Matthew almost fainted. "What do you have to say, Matthew," said the announcer.

"I..," Matthew heard his voice echo throughout the arena. "I think Sky Bordon is the greatest!" The crowd cheered in agreement.

Mr. Day just sighed. He waited for his son to come off the court. Matthew was expecting his dad to be as excited as he was. His father didn't seem that happy.

"We're going to meet Sky Bordon," said Matthew. "Aren't you excited?"

Mr. Day was about to answer when Joy Hansen walked up. She was still clapping for Matthew. She shook Matthew's hand.

"Congratulations Matt. I'm so happy you won."

Joy Hansen worked out the details of Matthew's day with Sky Bordon. Sky would go with him to school on Monday morning. In the afternoon, Matthew would attend a Stingray practice session. Mr. Day was invited too. He said he would not be able to come.

Chapter 9

The Sky Is Falling

Monday morning began with a long black car picking up Matthew. The driver opened the door for him. Huge, long legs were the first things Matthew saw. Sky Bordon filled up most of the back seat.

Sky noticed the blue paint on Matthew's shoes. "I didn't know Double Pump Slammers came with blue soles."

Matthew was embarrassed. "They don't. It's paint. It's a long story."

Matthew spent the whole trip to school talking about Sky's best games. Sky didn't say much. He just nodded once in awhile. A group of students waited outside the car.

"Why do I have to do this?" said Sky angrily. Matthew was shocked.

Sky stepped from the car, smiled and waved. Two teachers fought to clear a path for the basketball player. Matthew got lost in the crowd as the children followed Sky.

He walked into the school alone. "There you are," said the principal.

He grabbed Matthew's hand and led him to the gym. The teachers had gotten the children to sit with their classes. It almost seemed silly that everyone was making such a fuss.

The principal got everyone quiet. "Sky is going to show us how to make baskets!"

The students clapped their hands. Some whistled. Their teachers gave them a stern look.

Sky dribbled a basketball. He put his arm on Matthew's shoulder. Matthew was in front of everyone in the school. Still, he felt he was invisible. Everyone was watching Sky.

"My buddy, Mark here is going to help me."

"Matt," corrected Matthew.

"Right, my buddy Matt is going to help me."

Sky gave Matthew the ball. Matthew dribbled toward the basket. Sky slapped the ball away. He sprinted down the court for a slam-dunk.

"Matt has shown you the wrong way to

dribble," said Sky. Everyone laughed.

Matthew was embarrassed. Play after play, Sky used Matthew as an example. That is, an example of the wrong way to play. Everyone laughed at Matthew shooting, defending, and dribbling. It was the longest morning of his life.

At lunch, everyone was around Sky seeking autographs. They all told him what a great

basketball player he was. Matthew was getting bored at hearing it all. He picked up his trash and walked to the trashcan.

When he got back to the table, Sky was gone. A teacher came up to him. "Sky is waiting for you in the car. Tell us all about the practice tomorrow."

Matthew walked slowly to the car. The window was rolled down. Sky was talking on a cell phone.

"Let me talk to the owner of the Cougars." Sky was almost yelling.

"Cougars?" thought Matthew, "Why would he talk to the Cougars?"

The Stingrays only had a two game lead on the Cougars. Sky saw Matthew.

"Uh...kid, I have some business to take care of. I'm going to have to cancel out on you." He went back to talking on the cell phone.

Matthew walked back toward the school. He watched as the black car sped away.

"I didn't want to go anyway." He yelled at the car.

That evening, Stingray fans across the city were shocked.

"Superstar Sky Bordon was traded to the Cougars today. An inside source has revealed that Sky demanded to be traded." The broadcaster on the news looked sad.

Mr. Day looked at Matthew. "That's quite a blow to the Stingrays."

"It's no big loss," said Matthew. He walked to his room. A few minutes later his dad knocked on the door.

"Come in," said Matthew.

Matthew was holding his scripture board. *"1 John 5:21, Children keep yourselves away from idols,"* said Matthew. "Can a person be an idol?" he asked his dad.

"I guess so if you pay too much attention to him or her."

"I'm so stupid, why can't I be more like you. I can't imagine you chasing after some silly basketball player," said Matthew.

His father shook his head. "I'm worse. I was jealous of some silly basketball player."

"Jealous?" asked Matthew.

Mr. Day grabbed the memory verse board. "I wanted to be your idol instead of Sky Bordon."

Matthew nodded, "Oh, that's why you've been acting so weird. Well, you are my idol, kind of..."

"Matthew, you don't need an idol. I'm not worthy to be an idol. But I know someone who is worthy of your worship." said Mr. Day.

"Mom?" asked Matthew.

Mr. Day nodded, "No, she's pretty special, but not that special."

"Well, it's certainly not Rachel!"

"I think that's too much to ask of you Matthew," laughed Mr. Day. "No, the one I have in mind is Jesus. He's not an idol. He's the real thing."

"You mean Jesus will never let me down like Sky did," said Matthew.

"That depends on what you mean by let you down. Do you think He will always do what you want Him to do? If so, He may let you down. But, He will always do what is right for you. He will never let you down in that way."

Matthew forgot about Sky Bordon until a few months later. It was in a shoe store.

"Hey Dad! Over here."

Mr. Day stared at the life-size poster and laughed.

"He stole my idea!" said Matthew.

There was Sky holding a pair of Double Pump Slammers. The shoes had bright blue soles, sky blue!

NOW! WITH BLUE SOLES

Chapter 10

The Lost Sole

Morning came too soon for Matthew. His alarm clock rang for three minutes. Matthew groaned. He pulled his pillow over his ears.

The bed always felt so comfortable on school mornings. The blankets were soft and snuggly. A few more hours and Matthew would be ready to get up. Unfortunately, time was not on his side. His bedroom door creaked open.

"Go get him!" said Mr. Day cheerfully.

Buster jumped onto the bed. He was so happy to see his master. The pup found Matthew's foot sticking out of the blanket. The dog started licking it.

Matthew was very ticklish. His foot popped back under the blanket. Buster thought it was a game. He was ready to play. The dog grabbed the blanket and pulled.

Buster wrestled the blanket to the floor. Suddenly, all the toasty comfort was gone. It was replaced by the cool morning chill.

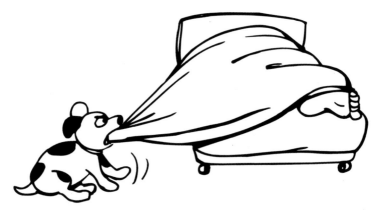

Matthew curled up in a ball. Buster now had a clear shot at both feet. Soon, all of Matthew's sleepiness was replaced by giggles.

"Don't tickle him too much," Mr. Day said to Buster. "That's my job."

"You've been replaced by a dog," teased Matthew.

"Good," said Mr. Day. "Buster can give you an allowance."

Matthew scratched Buster's head. "Buster, you're no longer my dad. You can't afford a son like me."

"Well, I'm off to work," said Mr. Day. "I've got to make some money to afford a son like you." Matthew's dad left the room.

Buster hopped off the bed. He was ready for a new day of playing. At the edge of the bed, the dog saw something that looked fun. He grabbed it and ran out the door.

Matthew didn't see the dog leave. He was rubbing his eyes. His mouth stretched in a big yawn. Matthew started to stand up.

One foot landed on the floor. The other foot hit Matthew's right shoe. He nudged it out of the way. That's when Matthew noticed something strange. The left shoe was missing.

Matthew hopped off the bed and looked under it. Nothing. Well, not exactly nothing. There were plenty of dusty toys and candy wrappers. The left Double Pump Slammer was no where in sight.

Suddenly, Matthew had another terrible thought, P.E. Ordinarily, the thought of physical education class was a pleasant one.

Usually the class played games. Today was the big race. The coach even had a stopwatch.

He just had to beat Buzz. Last year, Buzz beat Matthew by three seconds. Bradley "Buzz" Buzzell was the class clown. Matthew liked Buzz, sometimes. Other times, Buzz could be very annoying. Even when Buzz was annoying, Matthew still tried to like him. It was just more of a challenge.

Buzz called Matthew "snail boy" for weeks after their last race. Buzz wasn't trying to be mean to Matthew. He was trying to be funny. Matthew didn't think Buzz was very successful. If being funny was a school subject, Matthew would have given Buzz an "F". That would have matched Buzz's spelling grade.

Of course, that was before Matthew got his Double Pump Slammers. Matthew was looking forward to beating Buzz while the whole class watched. He had dreamed of this day since he got the new shoes. He was going to fly like an eagle. Good-bye "snail boy". Hello Buzz the turtle boy.

Matthew knew the shoe had to be somewhere close. He looked in his closet. No shoe. He looked under his bed again, still no shoe. He looked in the hallway. Not a Double Pump Slammer was in sight. He was starting to panic.

Matthew would need help. This was important. He knew the shoe couldn't have walked off by itself. The clock was ticking. He needed to get ready for school. Not only did he need help. He needed the best.

Chapter 11

Mom to the Rescue

"Mom!" yelled Matthew as loud as he could.

His mom popped out of Rachel's room. "Are you okay?"

"No," said Matthew. "I'm terrible."

"Do you feel sick?" asked Mrs. Day.

"Yes," answered Matthew.

"Is it your stomach?"

"Maybe it's his head," said Rachel.

"No," answered Matthew. "It's my shoe."

"I was right," said Rachel. "It is his head. He's going crazy."

Mrs. Day frowned. "You're not helping."

"I am too," defended Rachel. "He's my brother. I helped drive him crazy."

Mrs. Day tried not to laugh. Matthew didn't find it too funny. He needed his shoe. He needed it now.

"I can't find my left shoe," said Matthew.

"It didn't just walk off by itself," said his mom.

Matthew knew she was going to say that. He also knew what she was going to say next.

"It's probably right where you left it," Mrs. Day added.

Right on schedule, thought Matthew.

"That would be inside the front door," said Rachel. "Remember we almost tripped over them. That's when I put them next to your bed."

Rachel went into Matthew's room. She pointed to the spot she placed them. Rachel picked up the right shoe.

"Here it is," she said. "Right where I put them."

"I have two feet!" said Matthew. "I need two shoes. What did you do with the other one?"

"I put it right here," said Rachel.

"It's not here. You hid it somewhere," accused Matthew.

Rachel turned red with anger, "I did not. I did you a favor. I carried your stinky tennis shoes to your room. I probably even saved a few lives. Someone could have smelled them and fainted."

"They're not stinky tennis shoes," corrected Matthew. "They're Double Pump Slammers!"

"Stinky Double Pump Slammers," Rachel pinched her nose to block the smell. "In fact, they're double stinky Double Pump Slammers!"

"Okay, okay," Mrs. Day stepped in. "Matthew, you are responsible for your shoes. Don't blame your sister. You need to get ready for the bus. Just wear your old tennis shoes today."

"I need my Double Pump Slammers," explained Matthew. "We're having races in P.E. I need those shoes to win. I'm too slow in my old tennis shoes. Besides, my Double Pump Slammers have the lucky blue paint on them."

"I remember how they got the blue paint," said Mrs. Day. "You weren't lucky that day. Besides, we don't believe in luck. We believe in God."

"But, I run faster in my Double Pump Slammers," explained Matthew. "I can't win without them."

"It's the same feet. It's the same legs. It's the same boy. Your old tennis shoes are perfectly fine. Why should it make that big of a difference?" asked Mrs. Day.

Matthew didn't know how to explain it to his mom. She just didn't know how important

Double Pump Slammers were. She didn't know what it felt like to be called "snail boy".

She didn't even know what a snail boy was. Of course, neither did Matthew. Only Buzz seemed to know the meaning of snail boy. It just sounded so slow.

Mrs. Day saw the look on Matthew's face. She had seen it before. Somehow, Matthew's mom understood something. She understood that her son was upset.

"I'll tell you what. You get ready for the bus. I'll keep looking until I find the shoe. If I don't find it before you leave, I'll bring your Double Pump Slammers to school. You should have them in time for P.E.," offered Mrs. Day.

"Do you really think you can find it?" asked Matthew.

"Well," said Mrs. Day. "It didn't just walk off by itself."

Somehow Matthew knew she was going to say that.

Chapter 12

Busted Buster

Matthew walked to the bus stop without his Double Pump Slammers. His feet felt heavy and slow. He felt like a "snail boy". His hope was in his mom now.

"Race you to the bus," said Rachel as she ran by him.

Matthew ran as fast as he could. Rachel was waiting at the bus stop. She wasn't even panting. She looked at her watch and shook her head.

"What took you so long?" asked Rachel.

Matthew knew what the problem was. He had the wrong shoes. Of course, he didn't even think about Rachel. She was older than Matthew. She was also the fastest student in the sixth grade.

"You hid my shoe," said Matthew.

"Maybe you hid your own shoe," said Rachel. "So you would have an excuse to lose."

Matthew was ready to begin an argument. The rumbling of the bus caught their attention. It squealed to a stop and the door swung open. Rachel sat with her friends. Matthew sat with his friends.

With Rachel and Matthew off to school, Mrs. Day began her search for the shoe. She started by looking under Matthew's bed. She found a mess, but no shoe. That reminded her that Matthew had some cleaning to do.

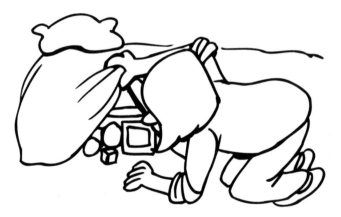

Mrs. Day looked all around Matthew's room. She looked by the front door. Matthew's mom looked every place she could think of. It was as if the shoe had walked off by itself.

"It couldn't have," Mrs. Day thought.

Mrs. Day walked into the kitchen. She was deep in thought. Buster was at the backdoor. He had followed Mr. Day out. Now the pup wanted back in. He wanted his breakfast.

"Oh Buster," said Mrs. Day. "Matthew got so distracted. He forgot to feed you."

She let the pup in. Mrs. Day scooped some Doggie Bits into Buster's bowl. Then she was ready to continue her search. She picked up on her last thoughts.

"It didn't just walk off by itself. Shoes need feet to move," she thought as she looked around the kitchen. As she stared at Buster, she suddenly had an idea.

"Maybe the shoe had some help from four paws!"

Mrs. Day walked outside. She looked around the yard. The shoe wasn't in sight. She walked to Buster's doghouse. The first thing she saw was a shoelace.

Suddenly she remembered the boots that Buster had chewed up. Mrs. Day was afraid to see what the shoe looked like. She pulled the shoelace. Mrs. Day sighed in relief. Buster must have been saving the shoe for an after breakfast snack.

The Double Pump Slammer was perfect. Well, not exactly perfect. It had blue paint on the sole. It was a little worn. It was also a little wet with puppy drool.

Mrs. Day took it in the house. She dried the shoe. Mrs. Day put it in a plastic grocery bag. She gathered the shoe's partner from Matthew's room. Soon, Mrs. Day and a pair of Double Pump Slammers were on their way to school.

Chapter 13

The Shoes On the Other Feet

Matthew watched the clock on the wall. P.E. class was only ten minutes away. Matthew still didn't have his shoes. That was the bad news. The good news was that Buzz was absent.

All that was about to change. At that moment, Matthew's mom was walking into the school. She carried the bag of shoes with her. The school secretary greeted Mrs. Day.

Five seconds later, Bradley "Buzz" Buzzell walked in. He carried a note in his hand. Buzz walked into the office. He was surprised to see Matthew's mom.

"Hi, Mrs. Matthew's Mom," he said. Buzz knew to call her Mrs. Day. He was just trying to be funny.

Mrs. Day smiled, "You're a little late today."

"I was at the dentist." He handed the note to the school secretary.

The secretary read it aloud. "Please excuse Bradley for being late. He had a dentist appointment. Please don't have him do any spelling today. The dentist said it was bad for his teeth."

The secretary looked at Buzz. "The first two sentences look like your mother's writing. The part about spelling looks a lot like your handwriting. Plus, you misspelled some words."

"What words did I misspell?" asked Buzz. "Oops!" Buzz covered his mouth. He suddenly realized he had told on himself.

"I think you need to do spelling everyday," said the secretary. "If it helps, you can brush your teeth afterwards. We don't want any cavities."

"I don't want to have to spell cavities," said Buzz.

"You can go on to class," said the secretary.

Buzz started to leave. "Wait a minute," said the secretary. "Is Matthew Day in your class?"

"Yes," answered Buzz.

"Could you take something to him?" asked Mrs. Day. She held out the bag.

"Sure," said Buzz.

"Good," said Mrs. Day. "Matthew was so worried about his shoes. We couldn't find one this morning. I guess there's a big race in P.E. this morning."

When Buzz arrived at his classroom, all the students were lined up. They were just walking out of the classroom. What perfect timing, thought Buzz. He missed all the morning work.

Now it was time for his favorite subject, P.E. It was the easiest school subject to spell; P-E.

"Go put your things away," said the Mrs. Anderson, the teacher. "Meet us on the playground."

Buzz hurried into the classroom and dropped his backpack at his desk. He picked up the bag of Matt's shoes. He started to run after the class. As he reached the door, Buzz stopped. He suddenly had an idea.

Matthew waited nervously on the playground. He kept watching the door. He was hoping to see his mom at any moment. She just couldn't let him down. Buzz was at school. Matthew just had to beat him.

The clicking sound of the door latch got Matthew's hopes up. Could it be Mom to the rescue? Matthew was immediately disappointed. It was only Buzz.

The P.E. teacher was already putting students into groups of three. Matthew stayed at the end of the line. He was trying to give his mom as much time as possible. Buzz joined the group. He stood behind Stacy Lane.

Stacy was the prettiest girl in class. At least, that's what Matthew thought. He wouldn't admit that she was pretty. People might get the idea that he was in love or something silly like that. He'd almost rather be called "snail boy".

"We're going to have the last group go first this morning," said the P.E. teacher. "I need Bradley, Matt, and Stacy to get on the track."

"Oh no," thought Matthew. He had to race Buzz again. He needed those Double Pump Slammers. Where was his mom? He was going to lose and it was all his mom's fault!

Matthew was getting upset at his mother. The three students walked to the line. The P.E. teacher held a clipboard and a stopwatch. He had the students do a few stretching exercises.

The three students stood at the line. Matthew was in the middle. He looked at Stacy. She gave him a smile. That made Matthew even more nervous.

"Good luck, Matt," said Stacy.

"Thanks," said Matthew. "You too."

Then Matthew looked at Buzz. He looked confident. Buzz looked like he was ready to win. He was ready to race.

"You'll need luck, snail boy," teased Buzz.

Matthew looked down at his shoes. They were his old tired tennis shoes. He glanced at Buzz's feet. Now there was a pair of shoes. He was doomed.

"Double Pump Slammers!" thought Matthew. "I didn't know Buzz had Double Pump Slammers."

Then, Matthew noticed the blue paint. There was only one pair of Double Pump Slammers like those in the whole world. Sure, there were the new Double Pump Slammers with blue soles. They were just imitations. The shoes on Buzz's feet were the real thing. They were Matthew's shoes.

"On your mark, get set, go!" said the P.E. teacher.

Chapter 14

Can My Shoe Lose?

Matthew was stunned. He just stood there. Stacy and Buzz took off. All the other kids were cheering.

"Go!" yelled the P.E. teacher to Matthew.

So Matthew went. He ran faster than he had ever run before. Buzz and Stacy had a big head start. Still, his legs pumped their hardest. Matt's old tennis shoes were flying.

He was determined to beat Buzz. Matthew

was in a race against his own Double Pump Slammers. The only thing that mattered was the finish line. He had to cross it before Buzz.

As Matthew drew closer, the class cheered louder. Matthew was a step behind Buzz. There was fifteen yards to go. In a burst of speed, Matthew zipped by Buzz. The class was going wild.

"The winner is...," said the P.E. teacher "Stacy Lane!"

Stacy came up to Matthew. "Thanks for letting me win, Matt. That was really sweet of you."

"What?" asked Matthew.

"I know you gave me that head start," said Stacy. "Otherwise, you would have won."

Buzz came up to them. "Wow! That was some race. You two are fast. You can just call me 'snail boy'."

"You don't mind being called 'snail boy'?" asked Matthew.

"You can call me anything you want as long as I know it's because we're friends," said Buzz.

"Friends? What about my shoes?" asked Matthew.

"Exactly," said Buzz. "You're such a good friend for loaning me your shoes. My mom made me wear my black loafers to the dentist. They're a little too big for me. They're hard to walk in."

"It's impossible to run in them. I'm glad you remembered I had a dentist appointment. That was thoughtful of you to have your mom bring the extra shoes. I'm surprised you didn't wear the Double Pump Slammers."

"Yes," laughed Stacy, "Double Pump Slammers make kids run really fast."

Buzz laughed too. "Hey, I'm the class clown. That was my joke."

"I don't get the joke," said Matthew.

"It's not the shoes that make people fast," explained Stacy. "People make the shoes fast. So, it's silly to think a pair of shoes will make that big of a difference."

"As long as you're not wearing loafers that are too big," added Buzz.

Matthew and Buzz walked to the buses after school. They walked slowly. Buzz was wearing his too-big loafers. Matthew could see why Buzz didn't want to run in them. They reached Matthew's bus first.

"Bye Matt," said Buzz.

"Bye 'snail boy'," said Matthew.

Matthew walked up the steps. There was only one place left to sit. Rachel had been late getting to the bus, too. Matthew would have to sit with his sister on the ride home.

"Did you just call Buzz, 'snail boy'?" asked Rachel.

"It's a long story. I beat him in a race today. Don't worry, he likes it," answered Matthew.

"Why wouldn't he?" laughed Rachel. "It's a nice change from 'Buzz'. I see you have your

Double Pump Slammers. Was that the key to your victory?"

"The key to my what?" asked Matthew. "I don't speak sixth-grade. Can you ask that in English?"

"I mean, is that the reason you won?" asked Rachel.

"No. I wore my old tennis shoes. Buzz borrowed the Double Pump Slammers."

"You said you needed the Double Pump Slammers to win. What happened?" asked Rachel.

"I just ran as fast as I could," said Matthew. "I even gave Buzz and Stacy Lane a head start. I beat Buzz and almost beat Stacy."

"So you gave Stacy a head start too? That was sweet of you," teased Rachel.

"I wasn't being sweet," argued Matthew.

"That reminds me of something in the Bible," said Rachel.

"Oh, I know," said Matthew. "We should run the race to win. That's in First Corinthians."

"Not the race," said Rachel. "The fact that you loaned Buzz your shoes. I know how important they are to you. Jesus says that we should be generous with the things we have. You should know that. After all, it is in the book of Matthew. Chapter five, I think."

Matthew was silent for a moment. "I didn't exactly loan Buzz my shoes. He borrowed them without asking. I'm actually glad he didn't ask. I probably would have said no. I thought I needed the Double Pump Slammers to beat Buzz."

"But you didn't need the shoes to beat Buzz," said Rachel.

"I didn't even need to beat Buzz at all," said Matthew. "I'm glad Jesus had me be generous, even if it was an accident."

"Accident?" asked Rachel. "It seems to me

like Jesus was teaching you something."

"If you let girls beat you, they'll think you're sweet?" asked Matthew.

"No," said Rachel. "He's teaching you to

care more about people than things."

Matthew smiled. "I think you're right. Buzz is more important to me than winning a race. My friends are more important than a pair of Double Pump Slammers."

"They are pretty smelly," said Rachel.

"My friends?" asked Matthew.

"No," laughed Rachel. "Those Double Pump Stinkers."

"You mean Slammers," corrected Matthew.

"My nose says stinkers," answered Rachel. "By the way, what does 'snail boy' mean."

"I'm not sure," said Matthew. "I think it means 'very good friend'."

"I've got to learn how to speak third-grade. It sounds like a fun language," laughed Rachel.

The Book of Matt is a chapter book series from McRuffy Press that emphasizes Christian values in a fresh and creative way.

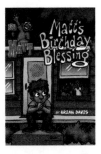

Matt's Birthday Blessing

Turning nine is just fine with Matthew Day. He's picked out a special birthday presnt, and knows how to get it. With God on his side, he can't go wrong. Or can he be?

ISBN 1-59269-056-4

My Shoes Got the Blues

What do a bulldog, a basketall star, and a big race have in common? They're all reasons Matthew's shoes have the blues. His Double Pump Slammers will never be the same.

ISBN 1-59269-057-2

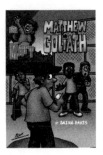

Matthew and Goliath

Big problems somtimes need small solutions. When Nathan Goliath moves to town, there's nothing but trouble, big trouble. Can one small boy stop the bullying?

ISBN 1-59269-058-0